GOOMER

Story by Dorothy Waldman
Pictures by Marie C. Nichols

ARIEL BOOKS
NEW YORK

ARIEL BOOKS

IS A DIVISION OF

PELLEGRINI & CUDAHY

MANUFACTURED IN THE UNITED STATES OF AMERICA

PUBLISHED SIMULTANEOUSLY IN CANADA

BY GEORGE J. MCLEOD, LTD., TORONTO

GETTING GOOMER

Goomer was a Siamese kitten who belonged to the Mr. and Mrs.. Like most of her kind, she was very different from ordinary cats. The things she thought up to do would be hard to believe.

When the Mr. and Mrs. took her from the house where she was born, she was seven weeks old. She and her two sisters were playing hide-and-seek in the living room the day the two grown-ups came in to choose a kitten. The mother, whose name was Lu Lu Liang, was lying in front of a big picture window, carefully washing herself.

Goomer didn't particularly care for the Mr. and Mrs. at first.
The Mr. looked big and stern. One sister seemed to like
them, though, for as soon as they entered the room, she went
into her act. She romped and played and rubbed against them.
Meanwhile, the other two kittens minded their own business
and gave her a chance to make her impression.

In spite of this exhibition, the Mrs. ignored her. Instead,
she picked up the smallest kitten and stroked her.

"This one has the prettiest face," she said. "Let's take her."

"Don't you like this one better?" the Mr. asked, pointing
to the kitten who had acted so smart. "The one you like is sort
of puny. It doesn't seem very playful."

After a long pause, the Mrs. made up her mind. "This is
the one I want," she said, and hugged the tiny kitten to her. So
that was that.

Goomer felt rather sad at leaving her family, but underneath she was very excited. When they all got into the car, she wanted to ask the Mr. and Mrs. where they were going, and a lot of other questions. However, instead she decided to wait and see for herself. So she settled down on the lady's lap and had a nap. When she awoke an hour later, they were driving into a garage. The Mrs. carried her up a flight of stairs. As the door was unlocked, Goomer had a sudden feeling of happiness. She was home.

GOOMER'S NEW HOME

The kitten's new home turned out to be an apartment. At first she was a little disappointed. She had hoped for a yard to play in, but the Mr. and Mrs. explained they were to live there only for a few months, until they could find the right house for them all. Also, apartment life turned out to be fun.

There were so many interesting things to see and do, the kitten didn't know where to start. It didn't matter anyway, for the Mrs. decided right off what she was to do first. She showed her a sandbox and explained its use. As if the kitten didn't know!

The first evening in the kitten's new home, the Mr. and Mrs. tried to think up a name for her. They wanted something unusual like Neko, or Tick-Tock. Meanwhile, the Mrs. started calling her Goomer. Well, you guessed it! The name stuck! She was quite proud of it, too. She knew she was the only kitten in the world named Goomer because the Mrs. made it up. She also was given a nickname, "The Goom."

TICK-TOCK? NEKO? GOOMER!

"THE GOOM"

Soon after they arrived, Goomer went exploring. She had just begun wondering where she was going to sleep when she found a box that was filled with the most wonderful, soft white stuff. She crawled in to try it for size. It was perfect! She curled up and fell asleep and the next thing she knew the Mrs. was saying, "Oh look! She's fallen asleep in the Kleenex box!"

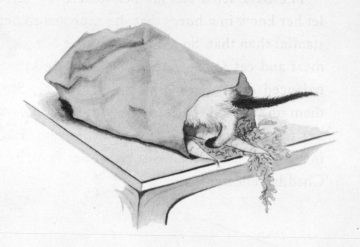

The Goom also learned to be careful about climbing inside paper bags because one time she got put away in the refrigerator with a bunch of carrots. It took her most of the afternoon to thaw out. She found, too, that a newspaper is not solid ground when it is sticking over the edge of a table or chair. Before she learned that lesson, she fell flat on her face several times.

The Mrs. tried feeding her some baby cereal, but Goomer let her know in a hurry that she expected something more substantial than that. So the Mrs. sent the Mr. out for some horse-meat and cat food. The young Siamese kitten had to have a balanced diet. No table scraps for her! She tried to make them understand that she liked an occasional raw egg to make her fur soft and pretty and that she wanted a bit of fish once in a while for dessert. Another of her favorite foods was sharp Cheddar cheese.

In the weeks that followed, Goomer had to grow up fast. After going downstairs several times with the Mrs., she learned how to do it without rolling all the way. When the Mr. and Mrs. had to leave her alone, Goomer learned not to cry.

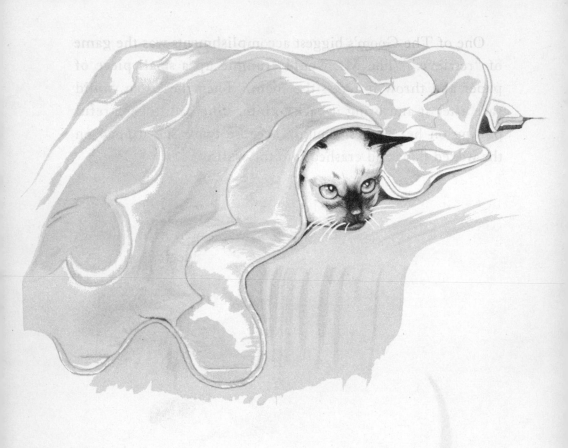

The Mr. and Mrs. had a small upright piano and they soon found out how much The Goom disliked music. When the Mrs. played or sang, the kitten just couldn't stand it. She had to leave the room. Usually she went and climbed under the bedcovers.

One of The Goom's biggest accomplishments was the game of "retrieve." The Mr. would crumple up a small piece of paper and throw it across the room. Then the kitten would race after it and bring it back to him. She had to be careful putting on her brakes, though, because twice she slipped on the waxed floor and crashed into the wall.

Retrieve was no fun if it was made too easy. Sometimes
Goomer deliberately pushed the paper far under the television
set or the couch. Those were tough spots to reach.

Sometimes the Mr. and Mrs. opened up the piano keyboard
and threw a wad of paper on the keys. Then the kitty tried to
retrieve the paper without stepping on the keys and making
any noise. That was really hard.

After Goomer outgrew the Kleenex box, then a shoe box, and then a hat box, she found it was nice and warm sleeping on top of the electric stove. Every night the Mr. told her a bedtime story which went something like this. "Once upon a time there was a Siamese kitty. She had cool little ears and a cool little nose."

After a while Goomer rolled over and the Mr. rubbed her tummy. In a few minutes she grew very drowsy.

Every so often the Mr. forgot to tell her a story and The Goom yowled and banged on the kitchen door to remind him.

THE BATH

One of the best times in Goomer's day was when the Mrs. took a bath. First, the kitten had to find out if it was going to be straight or bubble. If it was straight, she caught herself forty winks on the nice, soft bath mat in front of the tub. But if it was bubble, she jumped up on the side of the tub while the Mrs. splashed the bubbles all around and threw some in the air. Goomer's job was to catch them as they glided down.

The trouble with the bubble bath was that the edges of the tub got slippery. At least three times The Goom fell in. She didn't mind the water. In fact, she rather liked it. What she hated was the awful soap bubble taste when she licked herself clean.

Soon after Goomer came to her new home, she had an em-
barrassing experience. The Mr. was typing in the bedroom.
She had been keeping him company on his desk, helping him
with some notes. This grew boring, so the kitten looked for
something more interesting to do.

She went into the bathroom and began poking about. The way the Mr. was facing, he could look up every once in a while and keep an eye on her. Suddenly there was a splash and Goomer fell into the You-Know What. The kitty was very humiliated when the Mr. laughed at her, but he quickly came and fished her out.

THE STRANGER

For a few days, Goomer thought the Mr. and Mrs. had two Siamese cats. The Mrs. had a full-length mirror inside her bedroom door. One day when The Goom was strolling by, she caught a glimpse of another kitty like herself. She took a dim view of this stranger.

"What are you doing in my house?" she asked.

No answer.

"Come on. Put up your mitts." Then Goomer leaped as high as she could and was surprised to see the other Siamese leap the same way. He was good and fast, almost as fast as she was. They bumped and he was hard as a rock. Goomer fell back stunned.

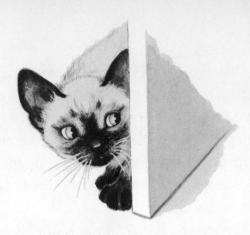

The Goom decided to sneak behind the door and attack him on the sly. Oddly enough, she found no one there and was feeling quite pleased until she went in front of the mirror and —there he was again!

"So you're still around! Well, I'll teach you to barge into a private home," she growled and started punching. It was a tough job as he seemed to know just where she was going to punch and kept blocking her blows with paws that felt like cement.

As a last resort, Goomer arched her back and bristled her fur. She danced a bit sideways and prepared for a final attack. She saw that he was preparing for a final attack, too. She bared her fangs in an awesome grimace and rushed for him. But instead of turning tail and running, he made a horrible face and ran toward *her!* He was one of the ugliest cats she had ever seen.

After that Goomer decided to wait in ambush for him. She waited all day. Then, feeling brave, she looked everywhere, behind the sofa, under the bed, in the stall shower. She couldn't find that cat. It was the strangest thing.

The next morning The Goom got up determined to have a showdown. The Mr. went out to the kitchen to put the coffee on before he began shaving. As usual, Goomer jumped up on his shoulder and rode back to the bathroom. When the Mr. started to shave, imagine her shock when she saw the other kitty sitting on his shoulder. This was too much. Pointing her paw at the stranger, she said, "Either that cat goes, or I do."

Then she noticed something funny. There were two Mr.'s! She meowed, "Say, what's going on here?"

The Mr. saw her confusion and laughed. "You silly cat," he said, "haven't you ever seen a mirror before?"

Goomer felt very foolish when she discovered she was the other Siamese kitten.

A WORD ABOUT PEOPLE

Goomer wasn't the least bit shy with people. In fact, she enjoyed performing for them. She had some favorite tricks for showing off in front of certain types of visitors.

Trick No. 1 was for people who loved and adored dogs, had no use for cats, and wouldn't care if they were all dead. Now The Goom loved dogs, too. Some of her best friends were dogs. But she didn't think comparing dogs and cats was fair. They both had their faults and their virtues.

For these stupid visitors, Goomer started Trick No. 1 with a bang! She bristled her fur, danced sideways and gave a blood-curdling yowl. That usually stopped whatever conversation was going on.

The success of this act depended upon whether the Mr. and Mrs. were in the proper mood. If they weren't, she got locked in the kitchen. Otherwise, the Mr. started the game of retrieve with her. They played this a few times to show the guests what a smart kitten she was.

About this time one of the ladies usually exclaimed, "Why, that's just like my dog Rover! How clever!" (Just like Rover, indeed! Goomer had seen Rover retrieve and he was terrible at it.)

Trick No. 2 was for people who ignored her. She attracted their attention by running up and down the drapes several times. Then she ran back and forth across the top of them.

For the climax, she took a flying leap to the television set below. There she balanced herself on the door and swung to and fro licking one paw. WHAT an unusual cat!

UNCLE RUBE

Once a week Goomer went out to see Uncle Rube in the San Fernando Valley. The Mrs. did her wash at her mother's and they spent the entire day there.

Uncle Rube was a big black and white cat who used to belong to the Mr. and Mrs. When they first arrived in California from Boston, their apartment was too small for a cat, so Uncle Rube went to live with the Mrs.' parents. He liked it so much he never came back.

One time Goomer stayed a whole week with Uncle Rube. She had a wonderful time. She and Uncle Rube got into all kinds of mischief. They chased each other up and down the venetian blinds and made a terrible clattering noise.

Then they played hide and seek in the china closet.

After breaking a number of dishes, Goomer ran and hid in the washing machine. Uncle Rube chased in after her and accidentally hit the starting lever. Around and around they went. They tumbled and turned and fell against each other until the Mrs. came in and rescued them. When they finally were shooed out the back door, they didn't really mind. Uncle Rube headed straight for a cool spot in the garden and Goomer staggered along behind him. It was time for one of the older cat's stories.

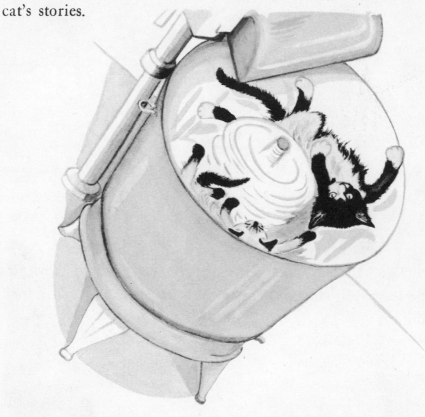

UNCLE RUBE'S STORY

It seems that back in Boston, before Uncle Rube arrived, the Mrs. always invited in any cat in the neighborhood whenever she could. And she had been trying to coax in an old battle-axe named Whitey for some time. She called him and called him whenever he came near the back porch but he never paid any attention to her.

The Mrs. particularly wanted Whitey to come in because he seemed so sad and hungry. Whitey was a very plain-looking cat.

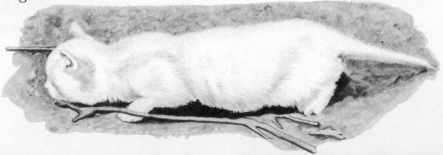

One evening while the Mr. and Mrs. were doing the dishes, there was a slight rustling noise in the snow outside the kitchen door. When the Mrs. opened it, there sat Whitey on top of a snowman the neighbors' children had made. With his white fur, sitting quietly the way he was, Whitey almost looked as if he was made of snow, too. The Mrs. picked him up and carried him inside. For once, Whitey did not protest or try to run away.

They gave him a bowl of warm milk and after he had lapped it up, Whitey curled into a ball in front of the fireplace and went to sleep. Lying there on the living room rug, Whitey looked perfectly contented.

The Mrs. sat and sewed, and the Mr. read a book. Whitey slept on in front of the roaring fire. Once in a while, the burning logs popped and crackled but the white cat never stirred. One time a large glowing spark snapped out of the flames and landed hissing on Whitey's paw. The Mrs. quickly brushed it off before Whitey woke up. Then she gently lifted the cat in her arms. She looked at him for a long time.

"Do you know," she finally said to the Mr., "this cat is deaf. Maybe that is why he never came when I called him before." She put her face down near Whitey. "The poor thing never heard me."

It was true. Whitey was very shy and sensitive about his affliction. That was why he did not seem friendly to people. After that evening, Whitey never again went into the Mr. and Mrs.' house. But every night before going to bed, the Mrs. put a bowl of warm milk on the back porch for him. And in the morning it was always empty.

After the Whitey episode, there was talk among the cats in the neighborhood that the Mr. and Mrs. might not get another kitten. But the very next day they went for a ride. They were passing through lovely country when the Mr. got the idea of stopping at one of the farms to see if there was a kitten around that no one wanted.

The first place they came to was the right place. It was thick with cats. There were cats who were expecting kittens. Cats who had just had kittens. Cats who were thinking of having kittens. Tom cats, mama cats, big cats, little cats, white cats, black cats, striped cats, orange cats. Cats, cats, cats.

And Uncle Rube was the lucky one. He was chosen to go with them. He slept in the sleeve of the Mrs.' sweater all the way home.

ACCIDENTS AND ADVENTURES

On the whole, the Mr. and Mrs. were agreeable people to live with. Sometimes, though, they were very inconsistent. They thought Goomer was cute when she played with string or bits of paper, but one day she got hold of the Mr.'s gold watch, and it was a week before she heard the end of it. What was all the fuss about? He got the watch fixed.

Then there was the time with the molasses. When the Mr. and Mrs. went out, they often were gone for hours. The Goom got bored. When she was tired of sleeping, she looked around for something to do. Occasionally, the kitchen cupboard doors were left open and she climbed up to see if there was anything interesting there.

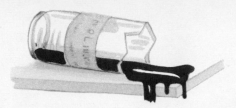

This particular night Goomer knocked down a bottle of molasses. It broke on hitting the counter and dripped all over. She tried to clean it up as best she could, but only managed to track up most of the kitchen. When the Mr. and Mrs. came home, The Goom didn't see what all the excitement was about. So she did spill a little molasses! So it did draw a few thousand ants! After all, it wasn't so bad for the grown-ups. They only had to clean the floor, but Goomer had to get that sticky stuff off her paws and feet. She licked them for an hour.

Then, one afternoon, the Mrs. brought home some yarn, and
announced she was going to knit a dress. She worked for hours
on it. She'd knit a couple of inches and then tear them out and
start all over again.

One night when she had about fourteen inches done, the Mr.
said to her, "How're you doing?"

The Mrs. answered, "Oh, all right, but even an inch takes
so long to knit! I should have started with something smaller
and simpler."

The Mrs. was so discouraged that The Goom decided to do something about it the first chance she got. The next day when the Mr. and Mrs. went off, Goomer dragged out that fourteen inches of knit dress and went to work on it. What a job! But she managed to put a hole in every inch! By the time she was through, she, too, wished the Mrs. had started something smaller. She chewed it so thoroughly that not even the yarn could be saved. It all came off in little pieces. If you don't think chewing holes in yarn is hard work, just try it sometime!

Unfortunately, another incident happened the same day. Soon after the knitting was taken care of, Goomer went to the kitchen to amuse herself. She jumped up on the sink and bumped against the cold water faucet. Instantly a stream of water came rushing out. What fun! Goomer had a wonderful time batting at the water with her paws, until she noticed the sink was overflowing. Goomer called for help but nobody heard her.

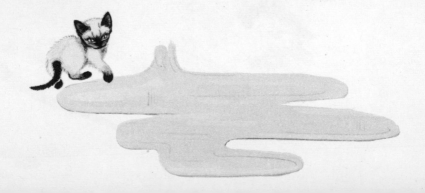

Soon the kitchen had nearly an inch of water sloshing about on the floor. Goomer kept hoping that the Mr. and Mrs. would come home. After what seemed like hours, the door opened. It was the Mr. and Mrs., and, *was* The Goom glad to see them! The feeling was not mutual. You should have heard the Mr. when he saw the water! The Mrs. just sat down and laughed. She thought it was very, very funny, and Goomer jumped up on her lap and laughed with her—until the Mrs. saw her knitting. Then *she* was furious!

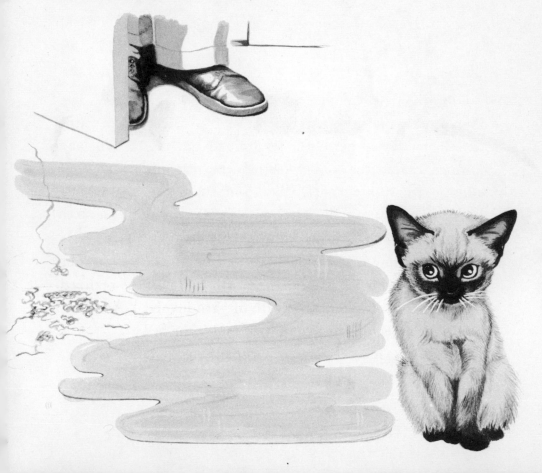

When the Mr. saw the knitting, he thought THAT was
very, very funny, and he sat down and laughed. So Goomer
jumped up on his lap and laughed with him until he realized
there was about five dollars' worth of yarn involved. And then
the little cat decided to go and hide under the bed.

That night Goomer got her first spanking.

HOUSE AND NEIGHBORS

Goomer had lived with the Mr. and Mrs. for a year when they bought a house. It was on a winding street, nestled at the bottom of a big hill. The hill was full of interesting caves and places to explore and Goomer felt it was all hers. The Mr. and Mrs. named the hill "Mount Goomer."

Goomer had never been so excited as the day she moved into her new home. While the furniture was being carried in, she went over the house, room by room, inside and out and from top to bottom in search of mice.

There weren't any mice but there was a great deal of other activity. The gas man and the plumber and the telephone man all were working.

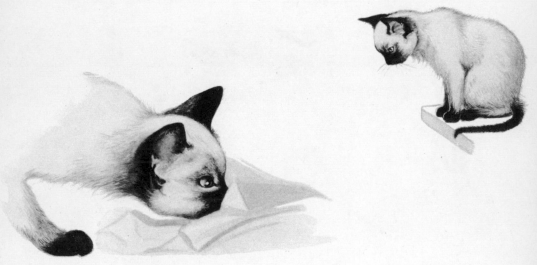

Naturally Goomer had to supervise each job.

But the most important job was the "cat door." A carpenter made a hole in the bottom of the kitchen door. Then he cut a little door to fit it and hung it on hinges so The Goom could push her way in or out of the house whenever she wished.

This was a good idea because then the Mr. and Mrs. did not have to get up every time Goomer meowed to go out or scratched to come in. Also, it made Goomer feel very grown-up and independent.

However, something unexpected happened. In the neighborhood of Mount Goomer lived many cats. There was a bobcat named Robert.

And there was Pepper, a lovely gray Persian pussy.

Then there was Slugger McDermott, one of the toughest cats in the neighborhood, and many others.

None of their houses had cat doors, so, of course, they all loved Goomer's. At first, it was fun just to push the door back and forth. Then they found that it was convenient and comfortable to call on Goomer when the nights got chilly and their own big doors were locked and their owners had gone to bed.

The Mr. and Mrs. awoke one morning to find fifteen strange cats in residence. Four of them were curled up asleep on the bed in the guest room.

Another, a large tortoise-shell cat, was playing with the Mrs.' perfume bottles in the bathroom.

Seven cats of assorted shapes and sizes were chasing one another back and forth across the sofa. There was even a cat in the linen closet and two others peeking out of the highest bookshelf. And, of course, there was Goomer, having the time of her life watching from a ringside seat on the mantel.

That evening the Mr. fastened a sliding bolt on the cat door, and from then on it was locked every night. But the Mr. and Mrs. reckoned without Goomer. For a kitten who could turn on a water faucet, a simple sliding bolt was no problem. While the Mr. and Mrs. were asleep, Goomer used to get up and let her friends in. Sometimes the cats played in the quiet darkened house all night. The Mr. and Mrs. didn't know it. In the morning, when they got up, the house was always empty.

It was the television set that finally trapped Goomer. The Mrs. usually turned it on in the afternoons while she did her housework. One of her favorite programs was sponsored by a company that made dog and cat food. During the commercials, handsome dogs and cats paraded back and forth on the screen. Goomer ws fascinated. She learned to wait and watch for them.

One afternoon the Mrs. came in to find at least fifteen cats seated in a circle before the set!

JESSIE

But there was one cat who never came around with the others. This was Jessie, a large, ill-tempered tiger cat. She was the bully of the neighborhood. None of the other cats had any use for her. In truth, they were a little afraid of her, for Jessie was older and more experienced than they. Besides, she had long claws and sharp, pointed teeth. Even the dogs on Goomer's street were afraid of Jessie.

Goomer and Jessie did not get along very well. For one thing, Jessie was always trying to take over Goomer's mountain.

One day they argued it out. Jessie sauntered over to Mount Goomer and she was in a nasty mood. She started taking it out on Goomer, but The Goom talked right back to her. She called her a cranky old woman, and Jessie slapped her face. So Goomer boxed Jessie's ears. The fur flew. It was mostly Jessie's. From a safe distance all the other cats in the neighborhood watched eagerly.

Then Goomer chased Jessie. They were running across the steepest part of Mount Goomer when The Goom stumbled and fell, turning a complete flip-flop in the air, and rolled all the way down. Jessie was home by that time.

Later that evening The Goom went over to Jessie's house to settle matters once and for all. Around midnight there was a terrible screeching and yowling. People got out of bed and closed their windows against the noise. Fortunately, it did not last long. Soon Goomer trotted home and quietly let herself in the cat door.

The next day The Goom was quite pleased with herself, but when the Mr. and Mrs. saw her, they were horrified. Goomer tried to tell them that if they thought she looked badly, they ought to see the other cat.

The Mrs. washed Goomer's scratches and brushed her soft fur. But it was the Mr. who had the right idea. He said, "The Goom can certainly take care of herself. Jessie will never bully her again. She's the Champ of the Neighborhood!"

How right he was! The very next night when Goomer's friends gathered for their evening visit by way of the cat door, Jessie appeared looking very subdued and wistful, trailing along behind the other cats.

Goomer saw her. She realized that Jessie had come as much to apologize as to join in the fun. The other cats watched Jessie carefully. Up close she did not seem like such a bully. Instead, she was just a sleepy, comfortable-looking, fat old cat. Jessie blinked at the other cats. Then slowly she lowered her battle-scarred head and purred a kind of hopeful, rattly purr. Goomer purred back. The circle of cats generously opened up to make room for Jessie.

When the Mr. and Mrs. came down to the kitchen in the morning, The Goom was curled up sound asleep with her head on Jessie's paws. And Jessie was slowly and carefully licking Goomer's fur. The Champ was being taken care of in fine style. From now on she was Queen of Mount Goomer and all she beheld.

EPILOGUE

Perhaps you would like to know something about Goomer's Siamese background.

Siamese cats originally were found in Siam, a country in the Far East. Many hundred years ago, these cats were valued highly by the people and were even a part of their Buddhist religion. Whenever the King wanted to confer a special favor upon one of his loyal subjects, he would give him a Siamese cat. For centuries these cats were trained and used as watchdogs. Even today, when aroused, they are fierce fighters.

At birth they are pure white with pink noses, feet, and tail. Three days later the kittens begin showing faint traces of black around their pink ears. In about two weeks they lose their fine, white baby fur and grow a coarse grayish coat. Each day after that, their ears, feet, nose, and tail darken slightly. Finally, at the end of three months, their coats have changed to a light beige. Siamese cats, blue-eyed from birth, are often cross-eyed. This is considered a sign of being very well-bred.

Siamese cats, like all other cats, do not like to be picked up by the nape of the neck when they are no longer kittens. Neither do they enjoy being held too tightly. Cats are their own masters, and never should be held against their will. Their friendship is sincere, but it must be earned through loving care and kindness.